CAREERS *in Your Community*™

WORKING *as a* HAIRSTYLIST *in* YOUR COMMUNITY

Don Rauf

ROSEN PUBLISHING®
New York

Published in 2016 by The Rosen Publishing Group, Inc.
29 East 21st Street, New York, NY 10010

First Edition

Library of Congress Cataloging-in-Publication Data

Rauf, Don, author.
Working as a hairstylist in your community/Don Rauf.—First edition.
pages cm.—(Careers in your community)
Includes bibliographical references and index.
ISBN 978-1-4994-6121-3 (library bound)
1. Beauty operators—Juvenile literature. 2. Hairdressing—Vocational guidance—Juvenile literature. [1. Vocational guidance.] I. Title.
TT958.R38 2016
646.7'24092—dc23

2014047666

Manufactured in the United States of America

Contents

Introduction

Being a hairstylist requires much more than having a love for hair. A successful hairstylist combines many talents. Those who succeed are artistic and business-minded, and love working with people. On the artistic side, some hairstylists say they are sculptors, painters, and designers combined. They are great communicators and psychologists. Psychology and creativity come into play together as hairdressers discuss the types of hairstyle that will make their clients feel good about themselves. Hairstylists have to be creative to come up with the look that is right for each client.

Great hair can do a lot to lift people up and transform people. It gives confidence, professionalism, and positivity. Looking good makes people feel good. It's no wonder that hair salons are a vital part of just about every community in America. No matter how the economy is doing, people want to look their best. The Bureau of Labor Statistics predicts steady growth for this occupation.

The artistic aspect of the job is as plain as the hair on your head so to speak. Hairstylists are artists, and hair is their medium. With scissors, clippers, curlers, blow-dryers, and other tools of the trade, they shape their masterpieces atop the heads of their customers. They have a keen sense of fashion and keep up with

Hairstylists depend on many different talents to succeed. They are a combination of skilled artists, communicators, psychologists, students, businesspeople, and sales professionals.

the latest looks. They know what's in and what's out of style.

Hairstylists also have to keep up their own appearance and put forth an image of professionalism. Their look can be an advertisement for themselves. They have to be strong communicators and salespeople to sell customers on their talents. In a busy salon, stylists interact with a steady stream of customers all day long. Being personable and friendly definitely pays off in this career.

Hairstylists often have to be savvy business owners, operating their own hair salons, hiring staff, advertising, and handling transactions. Turning a profit owning a business can be stressful and a lot of work. But working in a salon brings variety, with different clients asking for different services and looks. The career can also provide great flexibility—with top hairdressers making appointments according to what best suits their schedules.

The job stays interesting, too, because there are always new things to learn—new techniques, new tools, and new looks. Keeping up with the latest products and techniques sometimes requires a bit of scientific smarts. Hairdressers need to know how hair dyes will react, for example.

If you're interested in a career that is key to the community and combines many different talents, this resource will reveal what it takes to get into this occupation and how to succeed in the job market.

CHAPTER *One*

Grooming for Success

Keith Funai is one of the owners of one of the busiest hair salons in Seattle, Washington: Coupe Rokei. The place is literally buzzing with activity as stylists are clipping, cutting, and coloring. A receptionist is greeting customers and people are waiting for a chair to open up to take care of their hair appointment. Some are getting cuts, while others are getting their hair colored. Apprentices are busy—some are learning to cut hair while others are stocking shelves with hair care products. When the salon is at full tilt on super busy days, all the chairs are full and all the apprentices are assisting the stylists. It can be loud with activity.

Funai and Rory McGowan have owned and operated Coupe Rokei Salon in downtown Seattle for almost thirty years. They have been a vital part of the community, making locals look their best through times of prosperity and times of recession.

Although hair salons can suffer when hard economic times hit, people always have a need to look good. People need to keep up their appearance so they can keep a job or get a new one if they've been laid off.

Those starting out in the hairstyling field need to get hands-on experience and training from seasoned professionals. Beginners have to cut hair on many heads to develop their craft.

Many salons offer nail and foot care services as well. These include manicures (fingernail care, including trimming and polish) and pedicures (toenail care, including trimming and polish).

Funai developed a passion to cut hair because his father was a barber. As he grew up, Funai saw how the hair industry was transforming and becoming more sophisticated. He says that the famous stylist Vidal Sassoon has a lot to do with how salons treat hair and why he is a hairstylist today. Sassoon helped change the world of women's hair where stiff hairsprays and curlers worn to bed were the norm. Sassoon was all about the cut and shaping the hairstyle to complement a woman's facial features. He was about bringing out hair's natural beauty instead of "freezing" it into a stiff shape that you couldn't even run your fingers through. For many, hairstyling became an art in the era of Sassoon, during the late 1960s and 1970s.

Hairstylists in Every Community

Today hairstyling artists are in almost every community across the country. Like Sassoon, most hairstylists today treat hair cutting as a creative endeavor. It's not just a world of barbershops offering trims and buzz cuts. Walk into almost any salon in America, and you will find books with scores of possible hairstyles with different lengths, shapes, and textures.

Many salons are small with four employees or less. Smaller salons may offer the basic services of cutting and coloring. Those that expand and have larger staffs may offer more services, such as hair extensions, nail treatments, and facials. Those

To prosper, a hair salon may offer services that go beyond traditional hair cutting, styling, and coloring. Other popular beauty treatments include manicures and pedicures.

that build a big customer base offer haircuts and treatments for women, men, teenagers, and children. To bring in even more revenue, most hair salons today offer hair products for sale as well—shampoos, conditioners, and other beauty-related supplies.

Hairstyling (including nail treatments) is a $50 billion industry, according IBISWorld's Hair & Nail Salons market research report. More than 1.6 million are employed in this industry, and there are more than 1.2 million businesses spread out in communities in all the states.

Birth of Hair Salons

In the United States, hair salons really took off during the roaring 1920s. At that time, hair salons were in full swing with about 25,000 businesses operating nationwide. Jazz, a budding film industry, and a strong economy were some of the elements defining the era. People became interested in fashion, and part of that interest was related to hair design. Short bobs and finger waves were styles that were replacing the stodgy Victorian cuts of the generation before.

During the 1930s, the Great Depression hit, closing many salons. But many beauty schools opened, promising to train people in the skills needed to become a successful stylist. The platinum hairdo of Jean Harlow came into vogue. In the 1940s, salons were booming, and they became popular gathering places for women across the country.

The idea of the salon as a gathering place in the community has continued throughout the decades, and it may be another reason that salons continue to survive and thrive. A salon originally had nothing

THE ROOTS OF HAIRSTYLING

Hairstyling is actually an ancient art. Even the earliest cavemen may have been grooming each other. The ancient Egyptians and Greeks all had forms of beautifying hair. Eventually, the barbershop developed as a place to get a hair cut.

The ancient Greeks and Romans were well known for their barbershops. In many ways, the barbershops then were like the salons of today. At the height of the Roman Empire, barbers were well-respected professionals. Nobles flocked to their shops, which were often elegantly fitted with large mirrors. They were celebrated lounging places, where people gathered to share gossip and the news of the day. And the best haircutters of the time were paid handsomely.

After the fall of the Roman Empire, the barbershop was also the place to go for a bloodletting (removing the blood for medical purposes), have a tooth pulled, or other medical procedures. In fact, on the traditional striped barber pole, the white stripes represented bandages and the red represented blood.

In the eighteenth century, wigs became vogue, so haircutters had to be expert wig makers and stylers. By the nineteenth century, wigs were on the way out and barbershops began to grow and flourish. By the end of the 1800s, salons just for women began to open. They didn't immediately catch on. Women were accustomed to doing their hair at home.

to do with hair. It was a place where people would gather to exchange ideas. The salon was an invention of sixteenth-century Italy, and the concept thrived in France in the seventeenth and eighteenth centuries. At salons, people would usually come together at someone's home. In some ways, many of the hair salons of today serve a similar function. People in the community come together and talk about events in the neighborhood, politics, local gossip, and their problems. Salons are often a vital force in a town that help people connect.

The 1950s were a time of prosperity and "traditional" values in the United States. Many women were entering the workplace and they wanted to have neat, professional, and attractive looks. As the 1960s progressed, more women were being more experimental and trying new things with their hair. The art of hairstyling was truly developing. Salons spread into department stores and malls. The 1970s brought the disco era and more styles. Some labeled this decade the Golden Age of the Hair Salon. Things were going full tilt when it came to the hair industry, and all sorts of experimentation was taking place. The 1980s might best be captured by big hair looks. Jheri curls, rat tails, and Aquanet were introduced. It was an era of the business look and big money. This attitude extended into the 1990s, when the best stylists became celebrities in their own right.

Today's Hairstyling World

In the early 2000s, recession hit the United States, and people cut back on what they spent on their hair cutting. Still, the salons did not die off. People want

As artists who work with hair as their medium, stylists rely on many different tools. Curlers may seem old-fashioned, but they are still used in salons today to add volume, shape, and waves.

to look good no matter how the economy is doing, and in hard times, their looks may be even more important as they spend more time looking for work. Salons suffered, but since that time the economy has rebounded and the salon industry has again picked up steam.

Hairstyling is a hot career field. The Bureau of Labor Statistics (BLS) predicts 13 percent growth for this career between 2012 and 2022. The BLS lists the latest nationwide average hourly wage for hairdressers and cosmetologists on its website. The hourly wage may be low at first, but stylists who put in the time and effort to build their name and customer base can earn much more. Many hairdressers earn generous tips so that might not be calculated into the base pay listed by the BLS. Obviously, wages can depend on the type of salon. The less expensive chains might just charge $10 for a cut, but the most elite operations may be asking for $800.

In an interview with National Public Radio, Jim Cox, executive director of the American Association of Cosmetology Schools stated his view that the Bureau of Labor Statistics numbers seemed too low. He said that average salaries can be especially high at upscale salons, where earnings can be 20 percent higher than the average, again without tips included.

Successful salons today take advantage of modern equipment. They build up clientele and a fan base using social media tools like Facebook and Twitter. Some hairstylists try to work with celebrities to make a name for themselves.

Anne McGowan is a stylist at Coupe Rokei who developed her reputation working outside of salons. She spent years doing hair for the Seattle Opera. She's

THE MOTHER OF THE MODERN SALON AND THE FIRST "CELEBRITY STYLIST"

During the latter half of the 1800s, Martha Matilda Harper did much to create the modern salon as we know it. Born in Canada, Harper worked as a domestic servant for twenty-two years before moving to Rochester, New York. While a servant, however, she took an interest in hair and developed a hair tonic designed to be natural and promote healthy hair growth. After saving up money working as a servant, she struck out on her own and began producing the tonic full-time.

Harper then opened her own hair salon. She was successful at the business and opened more, but she decided that her best approach to expand the business was through franchising, or licensing branch stores. She trained those who opened franchises and reviewed each one to make sure they were maintaining quality. She also invented reclining shampoo chairs to make sure customers were comfortable.

At its peak, the company had more than five hundred franchises and a complete line of hair care products. Harper was a proponent of the environment-friendly "green" movement long before its time. Her products boasted natural ingredients. Harper believed that synthetic dyes and chemicals did the hair more harm than good. She became the top hair care professional in the United States, and her services were sought out by famous names including Susan B. Anthony, Woodrow Wilson, and Jacqueline Kennedy.

styled hair for film, television, and print projects. She's done hair for celebrities such as Eva Marie Saint, Jerry Seinfeld, Viggo Mortensen, and Toni Collette, to name a few. This experience has built her reputation and makes her a much-sought-after stylist for customers. From small communities to big screen productions to fashion runway shows, hairstylists are in demand.

CHAPTER *Two*

Buzzing Along in the Hair Business

Some people who get into hairstyling figure out that the career is for them as they become adults and decide what they want to do with their lives. Others seem to know that this is the career for them even when they are young.

Hana Schaplow is a hairstylist who wanted to be in this field since she was child. She remembers how excited she would be to go to the hair salon to get her hair done.

"I basically couldn't sleep the night before because I was that excited," says Hana.

She was so into hairstyling and the fashion industry that she and her best friend transformed her bedroom into a salon one day. With her parents' permission, Hana got kitchen scissors and towels to drape around each of their shoulders to catch the hair.

"We just went to town on each other and wound up giving each other probably the worst haircuts we've ever had," she said. "We had to get corrective haircuts after that in a salon."

Even before a person is old enough for professional training, one may gain some hands-on experience cutting and styling hair with patient friends and family members.

When she reached high school, she started giving haircuts to family members. She didn't have the official tools yet so she would just use common kitchen scissors with orange handles. Luckily, her family was patient and let her experiment and learn.

Testing the Waters

Like Hana, many hairstylists get started by trying to cut hair of friends and family. To see if the work environment is appealing, a person may go to different salons and try their services. Exploring salons in this way gives an idea of the many types of working

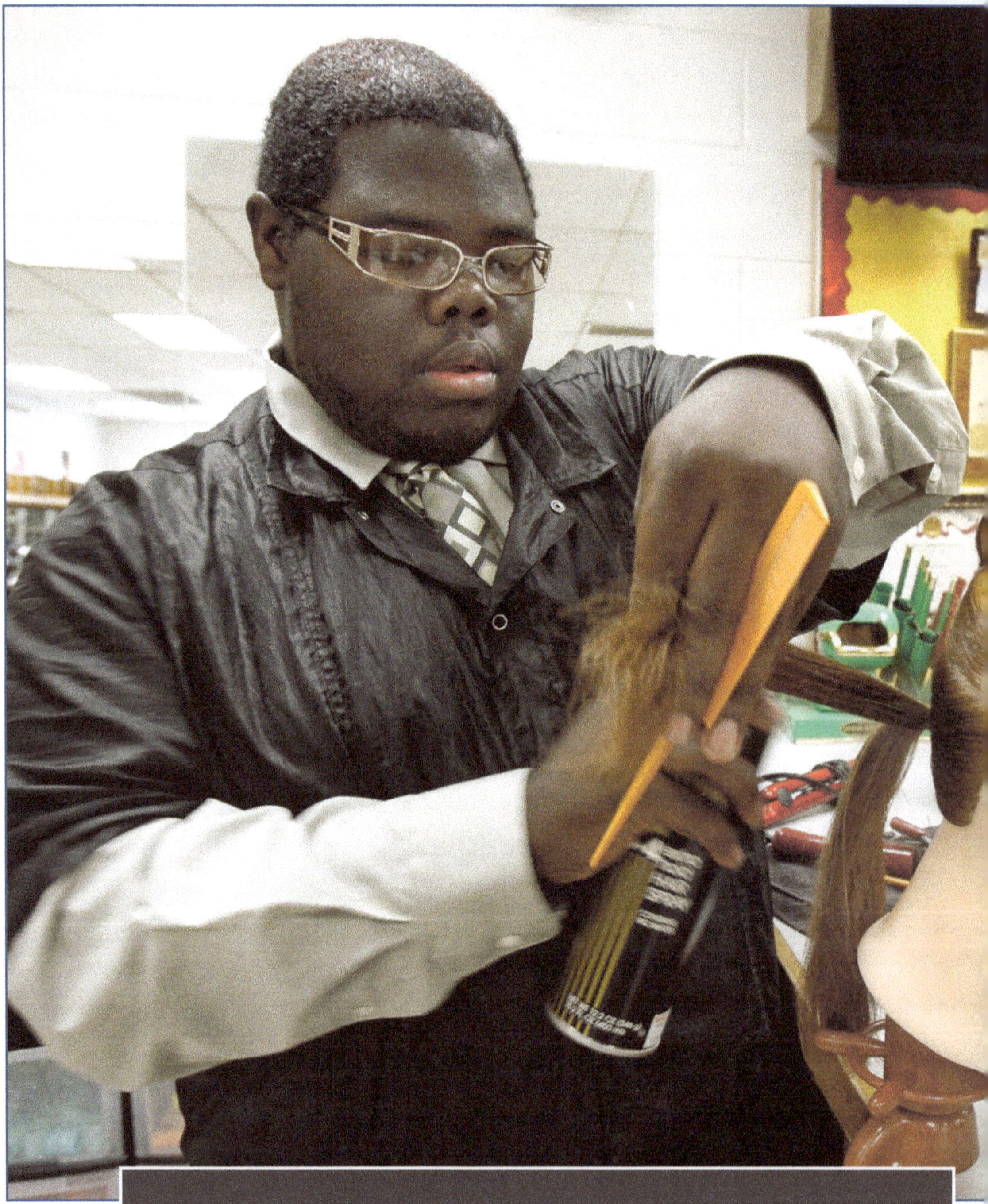

Some high schools offer programs in hairstyling. When he was in high school, Travis Thornton received professional training in hairstyling at Highland Springs Technical Center in Virginia.

environments that are available. Those interested in the career should go in for a haircut with a critical eye. Think if this is the type of atmosphere you might enjoy working in.

Some budding hairdressers take jobs in hair salons as assistants, receptionists, or general helpers who clean up and stock shelves just so they can get a close-up, insider's view of how these businesses operate.

By working in a salon in any position, one can get a sense of how stylists work together and interact with clients, transforming their looks with cutting and coloring. In a harmonious work environment, stylists often have a sense of camaraderie. They work together to have a successful business. When there are strong ties among workers, the employees often feel like family.

A productive salon is often a place of great creativity, and the stylists can be very satisfied with their jobs, combining a personal service with creativity. In a position such as receptionist, a person can learn how important customer service is to the career.

"You have to deal with all sorts of people in this business," said Hana. "I think customer service is something that everyone should have to experience at one point during their life."

Landing the First Job

To get that first job, hairstylists need professional training and to pass a state licensing exam. To find the right position, stylists who are starting out may tour many different salons to get a sense of what it would be like working at these establishments.

Some just starting out will job shadow at different salons. By visiting different salons, Hana was able to pinpoint the one salon where she really wanted to work. It was a five-star operation with its own advanced training program.

"The second I walked through the door at this salon, I felt like it was home," said Hana. "Everyone was smiling and looked like they loved what they were doing."

Sometime getting a foot in the door means going the extra mile and offering to volunteer without pay. It shows persistence and that you really want to work at that salon. By volunteering and simply being around, a person can show the salon what kind of person he or she is.

Getting hired can be a grueling process. A person may job-shadow for three months to demonstrate how well he or she meshes with the other stylists. An audition may also be required. Some salons require potential new hires to bring in a model and give a haircut that will be a huge transformation. An aspiring stylist might try to find someone with long straight hair that he or she can cut short and reshape. The salon owner would then review the cut. If impressed, the salon owner might hire the young stylist on as an apprentice.

Practice, practice, practice. Apprentices in this field need to hone their skills by working with live volunteers as well as mannequins.

Apprentices don't yet cut hair. They unpack inventory, stock shelves, clean the floor, sweep up hair, and shampoo for stylists. Apprentices often work for just minimum wage. Some salons require two-year apprenticeships before a person can advance.

A salon may also require its apprentices to bring in three models a week to learn their ways of cutting, foiling, and coloring and perming.

Finding that many models each week can be a real challenge. Sometimes, apprentices approach total strangers on the street and offer free hair cutting and styling just so they can have a model to work on.

TOOLS OF THE TRADE

In addition to scissors, here are some other essential tools that hairstylists depend on to make the cut.

Brushes. Brushes are often used in combination with a dryer to add volume. A boar bristle brush is a popular type.

Clippers. Clippers are electric or battery-powered devices used to shave hair. They are often used to remove large volumes of hair. Clippers usually have different attachments so the customer or hairdresser can decide how close to cut the hair. Clippers have to be properly lubricated to keep the tiny, rapidly moving blades moving smoothly. A clipper can be a trimmer as well, used to cut the hair on the back of the neck or neaten a beard of moustache. Some specialized clippers are for nose hair, ear hair, or eyebrows.

Combs. Along with scissors, stylists generally use combs to direct their cutting. Wide-tooth combs are often needed to detangle long hair. A rat tail comb is designed with a normal comb head on one end and a pointed handle on the other. The pointed side, which resembles a rat's tail, is used for making an accurate part. They can be used to precisely section hair being worked on. These combs are also used for teasing (also called backcombing) where the hair is brushed in a direction it doesn't naturally flow to create volume. In addition, these combs are often used for coloring.

Curling irons. This wand uses heat to change the structure and shape of hair. A curling iron does just what it implies—it can add curl or waves to hair.

Razors. Some stylists use shaping razors to add layers and form the hairstyle. Razors bring the ends of hair to thinner ends and scissors generally bring blunter endings. Experienced stylists know the texturing difference a razor can bring. Some use razors to achieve more softness and movement. Razors when not used appropriately can cause frizzing.

This type of training, which is fairly common at high-end salons, could be compared to a Ph.D. of hairstyling.

Apprenticeships also provide the new stylist with the opportunity to build clientele. An apprentice who has a model come in during his or her trial period might offer the model half price next time if the model comes back as a regular customer, or the model may like the haircut so much, he or she may come back as a regular customer no matter what the cost is.

If the model's haircut is spectacular, it serves as a great advertisement for the hairstylist. Others will see it and seek out the "artist." If the person who has a great haircut loves it, he or she will tell others. Many stylists say that they build a large portion of their customer base through word of mouth.

A stylist who needs to grow a base of regular customers might tell a regular that he or she will get a free haircut for every three new customers he or she sends to the stylist for an appointment.

Joining the Team

After completing an apprenticeship, stylists begin in earnest. They might start seeing clients five days a week or more. In the beginning, they may put in nine-hour days or longer to build up a base of steady customers. Typically, once a stylist shifts from being an apprentice, he or she no longer earns minimum wage. Many work strictly on commission and tips.

Stylists get regular customers who want to see them specifically, but they also offer services to walk-ins and to customers who couldn't get to see their usual stylist. Depending on how busy the day is, a stylist might see three to seven clients.

Hairdressers who take an active role in the community may find that this will broaden their customer base as well. They may do some community service. For example, if they provide some free haircuts for the elderly, they may find themselves generating a steady business with elderly customers. Giving back to the community that supports them is good for business.

Stylists often develop specialties. A stylist with blond hair might be familiar with what's best for blond hair and focus on that type of hair as a specialty. Another stylist might cater to the special hair needs of the elderly.

Cutting and coloring are standard services offered to these customers. Coloring has several different approaches, including highlighting, foils, hair bleaching, toning, and tinting.

Hairstyling is a people-person job. Professionals build relationships with customers and learn what looks will make them most satisfied. Here a stylist helps a client choose a flattering hair color.

Getting people to return as a repeat customer to the stylist chair requires more than just technical skill. People want to have a comfortable personal relationship with their stylist. Stylists are physically close to their customers, touching their heads to give them a new look. This closeness may open customers up personally as well.

"There's something about someone getting their head touched. Clients will spill their entire life story to me," said Hana. "They tell me the most personal things that you wouldn't tell your closest friend or family member. Some say I'm better than a therapist."

Never Stop Learning

Stylists who are popular have to keep up with popular styles and techniques. Salons want their stylists to be continually learning. At some salons, stylists gather once a month or so after regular work hours for in-house educational classes or to talk about the salon business—where it's going or what's coming up.

They might take classes in styling, coloring, or cutting taught by stylists whom they work with in the salon. Some stylists take classes outside the salon and bring that knowledge back to their coworkers. Sometimes educators from one of the big hair product companies, like Oribe or Wella, might come in to demonstrate a new product and teach how to use it correctly. Some salon owners reach out to the staff at fashion magazines and invite those experts to give a presentation. A stylist from *Vogue* magazine visited one salon sharing the latest trends from New York Fashion Week.

It's important that stylists keep up with the latest, hottest looks. They follow many of the fashion magazines and trade magazines dedicated to haircutting. In recent times, pixie cuts and hair painting were strong trends, but styles can change rapidly and hairdressers keep their eye on all media (television, movies, music, and fashion publications) to make sure they're informed and up to date.

Challenges and Rewards

One of the biggest rewards of this career is making people feel and look beautiful. Plus, there's a creative aspect of reinventing hair along with building relationships with people.

Bringing this lift to people is important in any community, and a stylist should be able to take this talent anywhere in the country if he or she ever wanted to relocate.

The challenges of the career may be biggest when a stylist is first starting out. It takes time to build clientele. A beginner stylist constantly has to promote himself or herself. It may mean promoting oneself through social media, such as Twitter and Facebook. These can be valuable tools for connecting with people and promoting services.

"Sometimes it can feel discouraging when you feel like you are doing everything possible to get your name out there, and you're still not as busy as you would like to be," says Hana. "It takes time and patience, but if you remain focused and determined, it will happen! For me it took about six months to a year to see my books more consistently booked."

Snip, Snip, Snip: Scissors Are a Hairdresser's Best Friend

Just like the painter needs the right brush to paint a masterpiece, a hairstylist needs the right hair scissors (also called shears). Scissors comes from the Latin word *cisoria* meaning cutting instrument. No stylist wants to deliver a hatchet job with poorly sharpened shears. Sharp blades are essential for precise, neat cutting. Many are made of stainless steal; others are coated in titanium to make them sharper and longer-lasting. Some scissors may be ice-tempered, a process that extends the life of the scissors.

Many stylists will have special scissors called thinning shears as well. These are used to remove thick volumes of hair when long thick hair needs to be thinned. Like a regular pair of scissors, they have two blades but the blades are jagged and have teeth like a comb. Blending shears are a variation on the thinning shears. Blending shears have one blade with a row of toothed-grooves like the thinning shears, but the other blade is straight like regular scissors. After shortening volumes of hair with thinning shears, a stylist may turn to the blending shears.

There are also texturizing shears that have even fewer teeth or wider gaps than thinning shears. These are used to create texture. Overall, the fewer the teeth, the more effect can be brought to the cut. Stylists often want to buy the best scissors they can because shoddy, cheap scissors can lead to shoddy, cheap haircuts.

Today's hair shears are designed ergonomically, with the science of the body taken into consideration.

Stylists depend on high-quality tools. Scissors, or shears, are one of the most important instruments in this trade. They should be well-sharpened and well-manufactured to give a stellar cut.

Styling scissors of today are intended not to strain the hand as much or bring on carpal tunnel syndrome.

Note also that scissors are designed to be right- or left-handed. So lefties need to consider getting cutters specifically created for the way their hands are oriented.

Stylists need to be aware when their scissors are working right. When they pull or push hair, a sharpening may be in order. If the shears aren't sliding through the hair as they cut, they may be getting dull. The screw connecting the two sides of the scissors has to be the perfect tightness as well. Hairdressers have to make sure their scissors are clean as well to protect their customers and keep them germ free. Some barbers use a disinfectant called Barbicide, but too much can ruin scissors. Cleaning shears with warm soapy water or alcohol works well, and then they should be dried with a soft towel.

CHAPTER Three

Making the Cut

A lot of hairstylists become interested in styling hair at a young age. They're interested in beauty, fashion, and trends. Some start to learn the skills by practicing on patient and trusting friends (who are willing to take a risk even if a cut goes a bit wrong).

Brittany, who is a stylist at the Purelux Salon in Arvada, Colorado, writes on her bio page on the salon website that she got started cutting and coloring her friends' hair at age twelve. Certainly, hands-on experience like this is valuable, but today's world of hairstyling is a fine art and requires very specific training. Instructors at cosmetology schools, community colleges, and vocational schools train those entering the field in all skills necessary to succeed.

Before heading into a hairstylist training program, it's a smart idea to explore the career on your own. Make sure this is the right path for you by visiting local salons. Look at them with a critical eye—what do you like and dislike. Ask a salon employee if you might arrange an informational interview. This is an informal but focused chat to gain a person's insight on a job. Find out likes, dislikes, and challenges. A part-time job at a salon may be helpful, too. That type of experience can give an inside view of what it's really like to work in this business. Even if the job is just sweeping up or answering phones, it's an opportunity to learn more about the challenges and rewards of the business.

Official Training

Many of today's salons and customers expect stylists to have official training. Stylist hopefuls can enter training programs at a young age. Schools often accept students starting at age sixteen. Most programs are geared toward helping individuals pass state licensing requirements. To be accepted into a program, you may have to pass placement tests. Many schools want their students to have sufficient math and English skills to enter their program.

One option is to enroll in a cosmetology or beauty school. A typical training program may be thirteen months. Schools often offer flexible schedules to accommodate students who may have to work part-time or full-time, or have family commitments. For example, a student might take classes for ten to twelve hours three days a week.

Classes will teach skills needed for the trade—cutting, coloring, perming, and relaxing hair. Schools typically give students hands-on experience with real volunteers. Students often have to recruit their own models to practice. When real-live people are not available, they may practice on mannequin heads.

Copiah-Lincoln Community College in Wesson, Mississippi, requires students to complete an application and provide a transcript from an accredited high school showing graduation or satisfactory scores on the GED test and/or a transcript from a previous college. Some schools

Hairstylists must pass a state licensing exam, which is controlled by a state board of cosmetology or similar agency. Stylist hopefuls devote much of their studies to passing these exams.

require an aptitude test to get in. The test may simply confirm basic reading, writing, and math skills. Some schools will ask applicants to meet with faculty members in person. A meeting can help them decide if a candidate is cut out for the program.

Keep in mind that all this training isn't free. Shop around before deciding on a hairstyling training program. Price should be one of the factors to compare. Make sure to include the cost of books and supplies as well. Check if a school offers financial aid—this can help bring the cost down. The federal government also offers financial aid in the form of grants, loans, and scholarships for many accredited schools. Look into applying and see what you may qualify for. Also hunt for private and community scholarships.

It's impossible to become a hairstylist by taking only online courses, but a student can get some training through this approach. It can be a more affordable and convenient approach then taking classes on campus. A typical course that may be offered online may review different types of popular hairstyles, along with some advice on how to create those hairdos.

A great deal of the training is dedicated to preparing students to pass the state licensing exam, which can last about four hours. The licensing exam has a practical hands-on component and a written part. Students often take several practice exams to make sure they're prepared.

Getting a Jump on Things

Some high schools give budding cosmetologists a jump on their career by providing training in hair design, skin care, nail technology, and massage. Lancaster High School in Lancaster, Ohio, and Cashmere High School in Cashmere, Washington, for example, are two high schools providing students with a curriculum in cosmetology. High school students can often start gaining the hands-on experience and work the hours necessary to earn

At some salons, apprentices who are starting their careers may be washing hair, stocking shelves, scheduling appointments, and performing other tasks before moving on to hair cutting.

state certification. In Washington State, licensing requires 1,800 hours of experience and training—that's the equivalent of forty-five workweeks of forty hours each. Many of these programs offer internships that place students in working salons to get real-life experience.

Cosmetology training generally takes nine months to a year and a half to complete to earn a diploma or certificate. Associate degree programs are generally a little more involved and take a little longer—two years.

IS HAIRSTYLIST A GOOD CAREER MATCH FOR YOU?

If you're mulling over the idea of becoming a hairstylist, you should take some time for self-reflection and consider if you are suited for this career. The quiz below can help you decide if you're cut out for cutting hair and beyond. If the majority of your answers are yes, this may be a field worth exploring.

1. Do you like to follow fashion trends?
2. Have you always had an interest in the latest hairstyles?
3. Have you tried different hairstyles and/or coloring techniques on yourself?
4. Do you love working with people?
5. Do you like conversing with other people?
6. Do you think you could work with some people you may not like and even be pleasant toward them?

7. Are you a good listener?
8. Do you enjoy multitasking?
9. Do you think you'd enjoy working flexible work hours?
10. Do you mind being on your feet all day long?
11. Are you good with your hands?
12. Are you comfortable touching other people's hair?
13. Do you mind working a job that is physically taxing?
14. Do you like things to be sanitary in the workplace?
15. Are you agreeable to working some days with long hours?
16. Are you willing to talk to others about what you do and sell your services?
17. Do you feel comfortable making suggestions about how other people should look?
18. Do you think you're able to handle people who are dissatisfied with the way they look?
19. Do you mind networking with others to find new customers?
20. Do you like the idea of running your own business?
21. Are you comfortable dealing with money?
22. Do you have some interest in chemistry?
23. Are you sensitive to people's needs (beauty needs, emotional needs, self-esteem issues)?
24. Are you diplomatic?
25. Are you good at reading people?
26. Can you give someone a cut and style that they want, even if it is in opposition to your own sense of style?

Schools equip students with all the skills needed to function in a salon. Through hands-on education, students master the basics of shampooing, drying, and cutting. Cutting techniques may demonstrate how to layer and create texture.

Learning the Science of Hair

Students also discover how to handle the chemical processes for coloring, bleaching, highlighting, and perming. Perming is short for giving a "permanent," also called a permanent wave. Prospective beauty experts learn how to handle the chemicals needed to shape hair. The chemicals break and reform the bonds of the hair. Specific hair shaping techniques are taught, such as razor cutting, braiding, and giving weaves.

When it comes to colors, a student may be instructed on how to use finely sliced foils across the scalp to add body. Or a beginner stylist may learn the technique of applying two separate colors to different areas of the same hair shaft. When used correctly, this approach adds style, color, volume, and texture to a hairdo.

Some of the more sophisticated courses cover human anatomy, facial structure, chemical processes, and skin reactions to certain chemicals and ingredients that are used in hair treatments.

Sanitation and sterilization lessons are crucial to keeping employees, clients, and the work environment safe and healthy. Business courses are typically included to understand how to hire staff and work in a salon.

Not all programs in cosmetology cover the business aspect in depth. Hairstylists can benefit

To succeed in the hair industry, business courses may prove helpful. These may include accounting, sales, and marketing. Marketing savvy can help create promotions like the one above to generate more clients.

from courses in accounting, marketing, and public relations. Advertising is often an important aspect to learn because salons in an area are all competing for the same customers. Successful hairdressers have to be able to stand up to the competition.

Hair and Beyond

Instruction may spread out beyond the realm of hair to cover some nail care (such as manicures and pedicures), skin care, and makeup. Students may learn special scalp treatment and how to permanently remove hair via electrolysis. Early on in the learning process, students may use mannequins to practice on and then advance to working on fellow students or volunteers.

Internships or apprenticeships are common for gaining the practical experience necessary to embark into this field. Working with real customers, students can see what the real-life challenges are like. This is a job that demands responsibility. Sometimes, things do go wrong with a hair treatment and honest hairdressers have to be able to own up to their mistakes and be ready to make the necessary corrections. On the job, one can see the great care and attention to detail that is needed.

Licensed to Thrill

Besides doing all this training to enter the work place, an advanced education in hairstyling and cosmetology gears people up to make it through the first hurdle: passing the state licensing exam. Every state will have its own specific requirements for

The learning never stops in the hairstyling trade. Professionals must keep up with the latest tools and techniques, and continuing education courses may be necessary for license renewal.

gaining a license—a total amount of hours of training required.

Apprenticeship time may be accepted as part of training hours. Hours vary from state to state but generally fall in the range of 1,500 to 2,100 hours. Hour requirements can be a lot less depending on the specialty. A makeup artist or nail specialist may only need 300 to 600 hours. An electrolysis (hair removal) technician may need 500 hours.

License options in this field are now wide-ranging. Illinois, for example, now offers a hair braiding license. Those interested in just skin care and facials would get a license to be an esthetician.

Learning doesn't stop after entering the work place. Once stylists are licensed and working, manufacturers of beauty products may approach them to teach how to use their products, such as semi-permanent straightening formulas, hair re-growth and replacement materials, and hair prosthetics (in other words, custom-made wigs that are often made for patients with a medical condition that causes them to lose their hair).

In some areas, state and regional licensing boards require that hairstylists take continuing education courses in order to renew their licenses so they can keep practicing their trade legally.

CHAPTER *Four*

A Growing Industry

The business of styling hair is growing. It may not be growing fast, but it is heading in an upward direction. In 2013, total revenues for all salon industry services (hair, skin, nails) plus salon retail grew at a rate of 2.7

Just like hair itself, the hair industry keeps growing. Communities across the country continue to need great salons that can give stylish and professional haircuts.

percent, according to the new "2013 Professional Salon Industry Haircare Study" from Professional Consultants & Resources. The total U.S. salon hair care market generated $64.8 billion in that same year.

While industry experts say growth is generally slow, salons keep opening in communities around the country. As of this writing, there were 301,000 salons and barbershops using and selling hair care products in the United States.

Cyrus Bulsara, president of Professional Consultants & Resources, said that one of the bright spots in the hair care industry is coloring. As the population ages, more people are going grey and looking to color their hair. Younger people are also more into experimenting with hair colors. Keratin and straightening services have also grown in recent years. Keratin hair treatments smooth out and straighten wavy or curly hair. Keratin is a type of protein that rebuilds, restores, and rejuvenates all types of hair. Some of these treatments have been controversial because some contain formaldehyde, which can be unhealthy. Cutting and styling services, however, have been growing more slowly than other services.

This survey of the hair industry also found that men are taking more interest in their grooming habits. The men's hair business climbed in recent years. Some salons also offer wig-styling, nail care, facial treatments, makeup, bikini waxing, massage, tanning, and other types of spa treatments.

Taking an Entrepreneurial Approach

Salons that offer a wide range of all these services are often called full-service salons. Other salons might just offer cutting and coloring, or just a few services. These are called specialized salons. Generally, however, the more services a salon provides, the more money it can make.

Some hairstylists will work for salons while others will try to increase their income by opening their own salon. Taking on the responsibility of owning a business, however, is a lot of work.

New business owners have to get their heads around cash flow. They have to know how much money is coming into their registers and how much is going out to pay bills. Some computer programs today are specifically designed to help salon owners with these financial matters (programs such as iSalon and Salon Cuts).

Many stylists run their own salons and have keen entrepreneurial skills. They've mastered the skills for running a business to build income and a steady flow of customers.

Although many salon owners may just want to offer cuts and styling, they may need to expand their services to survive and thrive. Waxing and manicures bring in a large percentage of income at many salons.

Someone who may want help opening a salon might consider franchising. Under this system, the owner pays a larger company for the right to use that company's name, system of operating, and resources (such as advertising). You could also buy out an established salon. An owner with a thriving business may be retiring, for example.

The Root of the Business

While specializing can be good for a career, most stylists need to offer all the basic services in a salon. It comes down to the three Cs—cutting, conditioning, and coloring. Just as painters know paints and sculptors know stone, stylists know their medium well—they understand hair. Basically, there are three hair types: thick, medium, and fine. Some women may have a combination of hair types. Then hair can have different types of texture. Hair may be wavy, straight, kinky, or curly.

The first step in the salon is usually to have hair washed and conditioned. It's easiest to work on hair that is free of dirt and grease. Customers often have their hair conditioned as well. Conditioners contain moisturizers that keep the hair more manageable and protect it from environmental factors such as extreme heat. Other ingredients strengthen hair structure and soften it. They contain restorative minerals and oils, such as olive, coconut, sweet almond, tea tree, or jojoba oil.

Hair coloring is one of the fine arts in this career. Hairdressers learn about chemical compounds to change hair color and how to apply them.

Sometimes, hairdressers will use essential, aromatic oils, extracted from flowers, grasses, fruits, leaves, roots, or trees, to nourish the hair and scalp.

In recent years, some customers have been skipping the shampooing and only having their hair conditioned. Some call this the "no-poo" method or co-washing (conditioner washing). Those who choose it are trying to avoid the hard detergents that can be in certain shampoos.

A more intensive type of conditioning is a hot oil treatment or deep conditioning, which is more effective at opening up the hair shaft and letting conditioner penetrate the hair.

When hair has been built up with various products and it needs to get super clean, a stylist may use a clarifying process using a special shampoo and possibly baking soda and vinegar.

After any shampooing and conditioning, the hair is rinsed out with lukewarm water. Hot water can cause damage such as frizzing and over drying. A professional may gently dry the hair with a towel, leaving it slightly damp. The hairdresser is careful not to over-rub the hair, which can create frizzing. The stylist may then use clips to work on one section of hair at a time.

To create a new look for a client, a stylist might experiment with where the part falls. Hairdressers have to master the blowout, using a round brush and dryer to give volume to a hairdo.

Making the Cut

When it comes to cut, there are scores of options. A customer may consider a bob, a stylish short cut that

In this business of making people look good, hair experts gain an understanding of the types of cuts that best suit different types of faces.

first gained popularity in the 1920s. The stylists may use a razor to give the tips a little flip. The style often features swingy layers (a layered bob). The bob can be an "A-line," meaning the hair is shorter in the back and angles to a longer front. A graduated bob (sometimes called an inverted bob) is similar to the A-line but it's layered and more curved in the back. With an asymmetrical bob, one side in the front is longer than the other.

When deciding what haircut is best for a client, the hairdresser will consider face shape. Faces may be oval, round, rectangular, square, triangular,

PERSONAL SERVICES

To bring in additional income, some salons are offering more services that go beyond the realm of hair. Some of the services are considered to be spa-style treatments—skin and body care, hair removal, and makeup. Here is a review of some of those services.

Facials. Massage, exfoliation, cleansing, and application of creams to the face. Blackheads may be extracted. A mask may be used to apply creams and moisturizers.

Waxing. A semipermanent method of removing unwanted hair. Wax is spread over the area to have hair removed and then typically the wax is pulled away, removing hair at its roots.

Electrolysis. Another hair removal method using heat from an electric current.

Eyebrow arching. Shaping the eyebrows by trimming and plucking out hairs with tweezers.

Makeup treatment. These services include cosmetics application, color analysis (to determine which colors of blush, eye shadow, etc., best suit a client), eyelash and eyebrow tinting.

Ear piercing. Cosmetologists may also piece ears for customers who want to wear earrings.

Massage. Some salons may offer massages of the back and neck to relax customers.

Hydrotherapy. This is the use of water to help people relax and relieve pain. Steam rooms, saunas, and hot tubs can all provide hydrotherapy. These options are typically found at spas but some businesses are combined salons and spas.

or heart-shaped. A round face might look best with a style that takes away from the roundness. Long layers that go beyond the chin can give the face a narrower look. With a more rectangular face, the goal may be to soften the jaw line with a bob.

The chop is another bob-length style with an irregular cut at the ends. The cap cut highlights bangs. The crop is a short-tapered cut. A person may also choose to go layered and mid-length, letting hair run down below the shoulder.

NAILING DOWN MORE BUSINESS

Cutting, cleaning, coloring, and treating fingernails and toenails has become big business, and more hairstylists and salons are expanding to include these income-generating services.

Manicures are the cutting, shaping, and often painting of the fingernails. They can also involve removal of the cuticles (the outer layer of skin around the base and sides of fingernails). A client may choose to get a French manicure, where the nails are painted pale pink with a white band at the tip. Specialists often treat the skin as well with a warm soak with healing oils and sea salt exfoliation, for example.

They may also offer a hand-softening paraffin treatment. With this application, wax is put on the hands, and even heat from the wax increases blood flow and relaxes the muscles. Joint stiffness and pain can be relieved, and a range of motion can come back to stiff hands. Nail wrapping is a technique for reinforcing nails, often using pieces of silk material. Nail specialists know all about acrylic and sculpted nail applications. Acrylic nail tips can be attached to natural nails to give the illusion of longer fingernails.

Pedicures are the cutting, shaping, and often painting of the toenails. Both pedicures and manicures can involve skin exfoliation (the removal of old dead skin cells on the skin's outer surface). Massages of feet and hands are often part of the process as well.

Some women like to add hair extensions, which are natural or artificial additions of hair that can quickly add length or volume.

For those looking to tame their curly locks, a popular recent approach is called the Brazilian blowout. The process involves a treatment with keratin (a protein similar to that found in hair) and a quick blow dry. Some call it a BKT (Brazilian keratin treatment). Sometime the process causes permanent relaxation of the hair.

To help those who want to keep their curls, a stylist might try plopping (or plunking). With this technique, a client's curls are basically "plopped" on top of the head and wrapped in a towel or cloth. It's intended to make curls bouncier, less frizzy, and curlier.

Modern Styles for a Fashion-Driven Business

At the time of this writing, fashion magazines were declaring the "updo" to be popular. This is a style where most of the hair is upswept and not falling freely, but loose tangles fall around the face. Models were seen with mixed textures, using hairspray to slick back the hair in recent years. Old world braids have come back in. Among African American women, bantu knots (a type of braid or twist) have become popular, and flat twists, coils, and cornrows remain in fashion. Some point to ornate ponytails and hair adorned with flowers or with gold accessories such as barrettes as growing trends.

In some areas of the country, the traditional "perm" seems to be dying out. Using chemicals, the process

Highlighting is one of the much-requested services in the modern salon industry. There are many types of lightening and darkening techniques to add interest to hair.

creates a "permanent" or a long-lasting wave or waves in the hair. A spiral perm is an option that gives long curls. With a spot perm, just a small area is given the treatment. In more recent years, some salons have introduced the digital perm, which uses a machine with a digital display to regulate the heat process. For the woman who may want curls or waves, the stylist may apply the curling iron.

Color Me Successful

Coloring is another service that stylists need to be up to speed and compete in this field. Colors may be applied through a foil technique, a painting approach, or another method. Highlighting uses a hair color or hair lightener to change hair tone. Lowlighting is basically the opposite approach, darkening strands of hair to add interest.

There are also glossing and glazing treatments. Gloss adds shine and tone and can last two to four weeks, whereas glazing is similar but lasts one to two weeks. To add a few strips of vibrant color, a customer may choose ribboning. Bleaching hair blond is another coloring technique. Haloing is a method for two-tone coloring.

Henna is yet another way to color. Henna is powder made from plants and mixed with water to make a paste for hair. It is also used as a strengthener and conditioner.

Ombre hair coloring has been popular and uses a technique called balayage—a free-form highlighting method. Ombre comes from the French for shaded, and in hair, the roots are generally darker and then the hair gets lighter toward the ends.

CHAPTER *Five*

Beyond the Salon

Today's world of hairstyling is highly competitive. It takes a combination of many factors to truly succeed in the business—drive, commitment, passion, hard work, strong people skills, and immense expertise in cutting hair.

Top stylists make a name for themselves. Those who get a haircut from a top stylist are often proud to show off their hairdo and tell who gave them the cut. It's a sign of prestige, fashion, and glamour. Some of the top stylists become celebrities in their own right, and they branch out into other areas where hairstyling is needed, such as movies, television, and fashion.

Sally Hershberger is a famous, internationally known celebrity stylist. She has risen to such a level that she has reportedly charged $800 for a haircut. Although Hershberger was born into a rich family with a father who was an oil executive,

At age eighteen, Sally Hershberger began working as an assistant in a hair salon. Today, she is one of the top paid stylists in the country.

she faced many challenges in her family as she grew up.

For Hershberger, hairstyling was not a driving passion since childhood as with some other stylists. In a way, the career found her. In the early 1980s, at age eighteen, she took a job working at Arthur Johns hair salon on Sunset Boulevard in Los Angeles. Johns was the hairstylist for the pop-singing star Olivia Newton-John. He was due to go on tour with her when he fell ill and had to cancel.

Hershberger was a fast learner so Johns sent Hershberger to Olivia as his replacement. While on tour, keeping Newton-John's hair looking its feathered best, Hershberger met the famous fashion photographer Herb Ritts.

Herb Ritts was taking photos of the top models and celebrities for the top fashion magazines in the country, such as *Vogue* and *Vanity Fair*. Hershberger's haircuts were being seen around the world and her client list steadily grew. She started working for other top photographers as well, like Annie Leibovitz.

Her next biggest break probably came when the actress Meg Ryan came for a new style. Hershberger gave her a choppy shag that Ryan sported in the 1995 comedy *French Kiss*. The look took off and became one of the most asked-for cuts of the decade.

Tom Cruise, Michelle Pfeiffer, and Hillary Rodham Clinton all got the Hershberger treatment. The first salon she opened under her name had an indoor pool and even a water wall. In 2005, she expanded her business further by launching Sally Hershberger FacePlace skin-care line and

Meg Ryan's shag haircut—created by Sally Hershberger—gave her a distinctive look that helped boost her celebrity status. It became a popular cut in the mid-1990s.

the clothing line Shagg Downtown. She plans to expand her haircare line, and she wants to get more into education, teaching aspiring hairstylists her techniques.

KEEPING UP WITH THE TIMES

Hairstylists are often on the cutting edge. It's critical for their business. Here are a few happenings in hairstyling that reflect the changing modern world we live in.

Computer-aided styling. Hairdressers today can go on a computer screen with customers. Some programs allow a photo of the customer to be digitally altered so they can envision what different hairstyles might look like.

Combining businesses. To keep afloat financially, some hairstylists have combined their salon spaces with other types of business that aren't the usual when it comes to hairdressing. Some have opened hair salons in combination with art galleries, coffee shops, and photography studios.

Green products. Like most businesses in the world today, hairstylists are moving to be more "green" and use ecologically friendly products. A lot of hair products get washed down the sink and wind up in our environment. That's why more products will list that they are chemical-free or use natural ingredients like olive oil.

In an interview in *Forbes* magazine, Hershberger said, "Know what you're great at and believe in it." She also advises tuning out those who say you can't do something. "I really don't listen to what people said I can't do. I listen to my inner voice." She advises people to be clear about their goals and be active in pursuing them.

For Hershberger, confidence is one of the most attractive traits that she looks for in people. She said that she is drawn to people who are smart, original, honest, and absolutely unafraid to be who they are.

Lights, Camera, Action

Like Hershberger, many stylists find opportunities outside of the salon. Movies, television shows, theater productions, and fashion shoots all require stylists. Hairstylists can also work on TV commercials and print advertisements. Some become stylists for fashion magazines. Hair experts may also find work with famous musicians or working on music videos.

Those who work in the entertainment business often collaborate with costume designers and makeup artists to make sure they're coordinating a proper look. If they are working on a period piece, stylists have to do their homework and make sure they know the exact hairstyles for that time in history. They often have to work with wigs to achieve the proper look. They may administer scalp treatments so the wigs or other hair treatments will not irritate the skin. They may be aware of a performer's allergies or other conditions that might be affected by hair applications.

Opportunities for stylists extend beyond the salon. Fashion shows, fashion magazines, television productions, plays, and films all employ hair professionals to keep their models and actors looking their best.

Hairdressers often take care of the looks of many cast members. A celebrity, however, may have his or her own person hair attendant. A stylist may have to stand at the ready to fix hair after every filmed scene. The same goes for stylist during a runway fashion show. When models change outfits, they often need hair fixed again for the next turn on the catwalk.

Fashion industry stylists have to be up to date on the latest cutting-edge trends. They have to take instruction from designers to achieve the exact look to match the clothes being modeled. It's important for all these hairdressers to build a portfolio of photos showing off their best work.

GLOSSARY

BANGS A fringe of hair on the forehead cut straight across.

BARBICIDE Popular brand name of a sanitizer used to disinfect hairstyling implements.

BOB A type of short haircut (mostly for women) that is usually jaw length and sometimes chin length. It often features bangs in the front.

CONDITIONER Often applied after shampooing, this product is designed to detangle and enrich the texture and appearance of hair.

COSMETOLOGIST An expert in giving beauty treatments, such as for the skin or hair.

ESTHETICIAN A beautician. Often this person has special training in administering facials, aromatherapy, hair and skin care, and makeup.

FOILS Small thin metal sheets used to separate strands of hair that will be lightened from strands of hair that will remain its natural color.

GRADUATED Also called stepped or shag, this approach adds volume to straight hair by adding many different layers. It is a technique that can elevate hair. A wedge cut and an angled cut are also types of graduated haircuts.

HIGHLIGHTS Strands of hair that have been lightened through coloring or bleaching.

JHERI CURLS A popular style among African American males in the 1980s in which the hair is treated to create glossy, loose curls. The product was created by Robert William Redding, also known as Jheri Redding.

PERM A hair process with heat and chemicals that gives long-lasting curls, waves, or other shape to the hair.

RAT TAIL A hairstyle characterized by a long piece of hair resembling a tail extending down from the back of the head.

RELAXER A type of hair product that loosens very tight curls.

SHAG A cut that is layered with various lengths of hair, giving the client a "shaggy" look. New York hairdresser Paul McGregor is given credit for inventing the cut when he gave one to Jane Fonda in 1971.

TEXTURIZE Adding texture to hair by relaxing hair, adding layers, or adding texture to hair with styling products and tools.

FOR MORE INFORMATION

Allied Beauty Association
7th Floor, South Tower
Capital Health Centre
10030 – 107 Street
Edmonton, AB T5J 4X7
Website: http://www.cabacanada.com
(780) 427-8517
Licensed professionals and/or students in the beauty industry can take advantage of educational programs, competitions, health benefits, and other programs that can help advance their careers through this organization. The group launched a new class of membership known as the Cosmetologist Allied Beauty Association (CABA). CABA's goal is to act as one national voice for all Canadian beauty industry professionals so they can reap the benefits of business programs and gain access to the latest trends, news, and events in the beauty world.

American Association of Cosmetology Schools
9927 E. Bell Road
Suite 110
Scottsdale, AZ 85260
Website: http://www.beautyschools.org
(800) 831-1086
Founded in 1924, this is an organization of privately owned schools of cosmetology arts and sciences, all dedicated to furthering the hair, beauty, and wellness profession. The group helps students find schools that are right for them, understand state licensing requirements, and pursue continuing education opportunities.

The American Board of Certified Haircolorists
P.O. Box 9090
San Pedro, CA 90734
Website: http://www.haircolorist.com
(310) 547-0814
This group of industry professionals has established standards of excellence for the field of hair coloring. Its certification exam tests stylists on coloring principles and applications, and gives the opportunity to demonstrate their mastery of this art.

Association of Cosmetology Salon Professionals
P.O. Box 207
Chapin, SC 29036
Website: http://www.mycosmetology.org
(803) 345-2909
This group promotes and supports professionalism in the cosmetology, esthetics, and nail industries. It offers many online continuing education classes for hairdressers and other salon professionals.

Beauty Council
201-3091 West Broadway
Vancouver, BC V6K 2G9
Website: http://www.beautycouncil.ca
(604) 871-0222
This Canadian beauty association has been setting the standards for cosmetology professionals since 1929. The council provides certificate of qualification exams in hair, esthetics, and nail technology, as well as other education opportunities and employment resources.

Nails, Skin & Hair of America
P.O. Box 679
Aiken, SC 29802
Website: http://www.nailsskinhair.org
(803) 226-0357
The NSHA pursues a mission to promote sanitation, education, and changes in legislation to enable beauty professionals to achieve the highest standards possible.

National Latino Cosmetology Association
7925 W Russell Road, Unit 401285
Las Vegas, NV 89140
Website: http://www.nlcamerican.org
(877) 658-3801
This association serves to provide resources for job seekers and professionals involved in the Latino beauty industry. Job assistance and networking opportunities are offered through its Career Center.

Professional Beauty Association
15825 N 71st Street #100
Scottsdale, AZ 85254
Website: http://www.probeauty.org
(480) 281-0424
This organization is made up of salons and spas, distributors, and manufacturers dedicated to improving their individual businesses and the industry as a whole. The PBA offers many online courses, classes on-demand, and webinars, as well as scholarship opportunities.

The Salon Association
11811 N Tatum Boulevard, Suite 1085

Phoenix, AZ 85028-1618
Website: http://www.salonassociation.com
(602) 996-0749
Created to help salon and spa owners, this organization offers tools and resources to help salon owners succeed.

Websites

Because of the changing nature of Internet links, Rosen Publishing has developed an online list of websites related to the subject of this book. This site is updated regularly. Please use this link to access this list:

http://www.rosenlinks.com/CIYC/Hair

FOR FURTHER READING

Academy of Freelance Makeup. *Makeup Is Art: Professional Techniques for Creating Original Looks*. London, England: Carlton Books, 2011.

CLIC International. *CLIC International Cosmetology Career Concepts: Practical Skills*. Montreal, QC: CLIC International, 2010.

Coffey, Tabatha. *It's Not Really About the Hair: The Honest Truth About Life, Love, and the Business of Beauty*. New York, NY: It Books/HarperCollins, 2012.

Entrepreneur Press. *Start Your Own Hair Salon and Day Spa: Your Step-by-Step Guide to Success* (StartUp Series). Irvine, CA: Entrepreneur Press, 2010.

Farr, Kendall. *The Pocket Stylist: Behind-the-Scenes Expertise from a Fashion Pro on Creating Your Own Look*. New York, NY: Gotham-Penguin Books, 2004.

Ferguson Publishing. *Cosmetology* (Ferguson's Careers in Focus). New York, NY: Ferguson Publishing, 2008.

Heos, Bridget. *A Career as a Hairstylist* (Essential Careers). New York, NY: The Rosen Publishing Group, 2010.

Milday. *Milady Standard Cosmetology 2012*. Boston, MA: Cengage Learning, 2011.

Morton, Rick. *50 Hairstylists*. Newbury Park, CA: ImagiMedia Publishing, 2008.

Newman, Marian. *The Complete Nail Technician* (Hairdressing and Beauty Industry Authority). Boston, MA: Cengage Learning, 2011.

Rosas, Peter. *Hairstylist How to Reach the Top: Your Success Is More Than Cutting Hair*. Cave Creek, AZ: Hairstylist How To Reach The Top LLC, 2013.

Schmidtke, Diana. *Shortcuts to a Successful Career as a Hairstylist or Make Up Artist in the Fashion and Entertainment Industry*. Los Angeles, CA: Lucy Girl Production, 2008.

Smith, Abby. *The Ultimate Hairstyle Handbook: Everyday Hairstyles for the Everyday Girl*. North Charleston, SC: CreateSpace, 2012.

Worthington, Charles. *The Complete Book of Hairstyling*. Richmond Hill, ON: Firefly Books, 2002.

Wright, Crystal. Crystal Wright's Hair Makeup & Fashion Styling Career Guide. 5th ed. Houston, TX: Motivational Media Productions, 2009.

BIBLIOGRAPHY

Beauty Rival Beauty Central. "A History of the Hair Salon & Styling." Retrieved October 20, 2014 (http://beautyrival.com/beauty-lounge/history-hair-salon-styling).

Buzzle. "Hair Salon Equipment List." Retrieved October 20, 2014 (http://www.buzzle.com/articles/hair-salon-equipment-list.html).

Caprino, Kathy. "Top Seven Success Tips from Celebrity Hairstylist and Entrepreneur Sally Hershberger." *Forbes*, May 19, 2012. Retrieved October 20, 2014 (http://www.forbes.com/sites/kathycaprino/2012/05/19/top-seven-success-tips-from-celebrity-hairstylist-and-entrepreneur-sally-hershberger/).

Chaves, Tricia. "What Special Training Does a Hair Stylist Need?" *The Houston Chronicle*. Retrieved October 20, 2014 (http://work.chron.com/special-training-hair-stylist-need-2988.html).

Copiah-Lincoln Community College. "Cosmetology." Retrieved October 20, 2014 (http://www.colin.edu/component/content/article/40-prospective-students/programs-of-study/183-cosmetology).

Education Portal. "Hair Stylist Training Programs and Requirements." Retrieved October 20, 2014 (http://education-portal.com/hair_stylist_training.html).

Employment and Social Development Canada. "Using Essential Skills: On the Job with a Hairstylist." Retrieved October 20, 2014 (http://www.esdc.gc.ca/eng/jobs/les/tools/awareness/hairstylist_story.shtml).

Encyclopedia of World Biography. "Sally Hershberger." Retrieved October 20, 2014 (http://www.notablebiographies.com/newsmakers2/2006-Ei-La/Hershberger-Sally.html).

Entrepreneur. "How to Open a Salon or Day Spa." August 30, 2005. Retrieved October 20, 2014 (http://www.entrepreneur.com/article/79550).

Farrell, Maureen. "How to Run a Beauty Salon: Costs." *Forbes*, April 23, 2007. Retrieved October 20, 2014 (http://www.forbes.com/2007/04/20/beauty-salon-aniston-ent-fin-cx_mf_0420fundsalonexpenses.html).

GCIMagazine.com. "2013 Professional Salon Industry Haircare Study Shows Slow Growth for the Industry." February 26, 2014. Retrieved October 20, 2014 (http://www.gcimagazine.com/marketstrends/segments/hair/2013-Professional-Salon-Industry-Haircare-Study-Shows-Slow-Growth-for-the-Industry-247270921.html).

Gilje, Shelby. "Cutting Cost—It's Hair Today, Gone Tomorrow, and Prices Bend Every Which Way." *The Seattle Times*, April 14, 1993. Retrieved October 20, 2014 (http://community.seattletimes.nwsource.com/archive/?date=19930414&slug=1695831).

Hairfinder: Hairstyles, Hair Care & Fashion. "Being a Hairdresser." Retrieved October 20, 2014 (http://www.hairfinder.com/info/hairdresser.htm).

Hillenmeyer, Jan. "2011 Salon Industry Study Shows Growth." *Modern Salon*, February 9, 2012. Retrieved October 20, 2014 (http://www.modernsalon.com/news/salon-industry-news/-New-2011-Professional-Salon-Industry-Haircare-Study-Shows-Strong-139012939.html).

MediaMatch. "Hair Stylist." Retrieved October 20, 2014 (http://www.media-match.com/usa/jobtypes/hair-stylist-jobs-402725.php).

Organic Color Systems. "8 New Rules to Make Millions in a Salon Business." Retrieved October 20, 2014 (http://www.organiccolorsystems.com/how-to-make-millions-in-a-salon-business/).

Purelux Salon. "Behind the Scissors with Brittany." Retrieved October 20, 2014 (http://pureluxsalon.com/about-us).

Timmons, Bronwyn. "Hairdressers'aTools." *The Houston Chronicle*. Retrieved October 20, 2014 (http://work.chron.com/hairdressers-tools-14810.html).

Weber, Bruce. "Vidal Sassoon, Hairdresser and Trendsetter, Dies at 84." *The New York Times*, May 9, 2012. Retrieved October 20, 2014 (http://www.nytimes.com/2012/05/10/fashion/vidal-sassoon-hairdresser-and-trendsetter-dies-at-84.html?pagewanted=all&_r=0).

Wood, Hollee. "Typical HAIRstyles for Your Face Shape." Holleewoodhair.com. June 26, 2012. Retrieved October 20, 2014 (http://holleewoodhair.com/2012/06/26/face-shape/4/).

INDEX